The Black Cowboy and His White Bride

Hunter Briggs

Copyright

Table of Contents

Chapter 1
Devil's Ridge, California 1867

William wiped his brow as he entered the negro only bar. Once he entered, several black faces stared at him and then settled back to their drinks. The bartender eyed him as he walked towards the bar. The saloon wasn't packed, with only seven patrons, a bartender, and a pianist playing a soft tone. All of them African. William was used to it. It was actually comforting to be with his own race. He found that there was safety in numbers.

"Whiskey," William growled as he sat on the stool.

The white-haired bartender grabbed a dirty glass and poured the brown liquid inside. William took a long sip and placed the glass on the table. Without another word, the bartender filled his glass up again, and William took another sip, drinking half of it.

"Where you from, son?" the older black man asked.

"What gave it away?" William chuckled, finishing his drink.

"I know all the negros in this mining town. You're the only face I don't recognize."

"You know all of them? Is that possible?"

"There ain't much of us out here, son."

"Makes sense."

"Name's Paul."

"William."

"So, what brings you into town? There's not much work for a negro here. Most railroads only want cheap Chinamen labor or Irish. Plus, the white man don't trust in the mines. Only jobs for us are servants."

"Didn't come for work."

He rose an eyebrow and held the whiskey bottle a little tighter. "I'm going to need payment for the next drink, son."

"I'm good for it." He muttered, taking out a few singles and placing them on the table. Paul swiped the cash up and poured another drink.

"So, what did you come for?"

"I wanted to see the Pacific Ocean."

"The ocean?" Paul laughed. "That's a good one. Seriously, why you here?"

"I wanted to see the ocean." William repeated, taking a sip. "When I served in the war, I heard about California from the other soldiers, and I promised myself if I survived, I'd make the trip."

"So, what are you going to do after you see the ocean?"

"I haven't gotten that far yet."

Paul laughed, holding his side as if William told the funniest joke ever.

"I like you, William."

William smirked and took another drink.

"Let me ask you a question. If your goal is to go see the ocean, why haven't you gone yet. What's the point of coming here first? I would have saw the ocean first."

"Last I checked the ocean ain't going anywhere, and a man has needs. I was thirsty, so I decided to stop for a drink."

"Good, lad," Paul added, topping him off.

"A man has other needs too..." William paused and looked around the saloon. "You sell pleasure at this establishment?"

"No, were just an inn."

"Any place where a colored man could get his due?"

"No, most whorehouses in the area don't allow colored men as it's bad for business."

"Figures."

"There is one place. You gotta go around back and pay double."

"Double!"

"It's a white whorehouse, but it's a bit of a dump. Most white men go there because the women are cheap and or ugly."

"A white woman? I ain't never been with no white woman before. What you trying to do, get me killed?"

"Hey, pussy is pussy. Those folks that run the place turn a blind eye for money. You can either go dry or enjoy your time. The choice is up to you. These white people don't care as long as the money is good."

William rolled his eyes. Normally he would've avoided the place, but his dick had other plans. It had been weeks since a woman last accompanied him, and he was desperate. With a sigh he said, "Shit, where is the place."

Chapter 2

William rode to the location that Paul directed him to. As he made his way across town, he found it interesting the color of peoples faces changed from black to white. Riding his horse through white part of town, he stuck out like a sore thumb as many stared at him. When he made it to the whorehouse, he could already hear and smell the sin. Women's shrieks and men's grunts could be heard as they pleasured themselves. William grinned and felt his cock throb from the excitement. The whorehouse itself was a two story brown wooden building. It had a wrapped around deck, with green shutters on the second floor.

Following Paul's instructions, he walked around back and knocked on the wooden door. The door opened and a large white man stood at the doorway.

"What do you want?" he growled.

"I was told to come here, if I wanted a lady."

He huffed and crossed his arms. "Double."

"Don't worry, I have the cash." William said, quickly, pulling out a wad paper.

"Pay now." He barked in a thick Irish accent. William handed the man his money and the guard counted it then moved out of the way. "Up the stairs, to your left. Look for madam green. She'd get you sorted."

A smile broke on William's face as he began to walk past the man.

"Wait! I need the gun, boy."

"Hold on partner, my gun ain't going off my hip." William hesitated.

"If you want to fuck, you give me gun."

William sighed and removed his hostler. "I better get this back. That gun was a gift for my service in the war."

The guard didn't reply as he walked away. William shook his head and then followed the instructions to go up the stairs. Once upstairs he heard several men grunting and woman moaning, and knew the rooms were in use. Walking around he wondered where he was supposed to be going when he spotted an older woman. She wore a yellow gown and stared at him.

"Madam Green?" He presumed.

"Can I help you?" she snapped.

"The man downstairs told me to come up here for a woman."

"You paid, I'm assuming?"

"I wouldn't be here if I didn't."

"Good. Follow me."

She led William to a room and pointed to the bed. "Wait here," she instructed. "Someone will be in here soon."

"Wait, don't I get to choose?" William asked.

She laughed. "You're a nigger. You don't get a choice. If my white customers find out that one of my whores had been tainted by a black man, they wouldn't touch her. You get broken in goods. Don't worry, her pussy is still good."

William rolled his eyes and sat on the edge of the bed waiting for his whore. In the next few minutes, a redhead woman walked in. She was a curvier woman, with a bigger breasts and a wider waist. William was stunned by her beauty as he observed her walking in. Based on what Paul told him, he expected a bucktoothed-ugly-wart-faced witch, but she was stunning. However, as he stared at her, he noticed the black eye on her face. His fists clenched seeing that someone hurt her.

How could someone hurt someone as beautiful as her? He wondered.

He stood off the bed, took his hat off and placed it on his chest. "Ma'am, my name is William."

"Mary." She stated. "Where did you want to do this?" Her eyes darting around the room.

"The bed is fine with me." She nodded and grabbed his hand, leading him to the bed.

She began undoing his trousers before William touched her hand. "Wait, what happened to your eye."

"This isn't about me. The quicker we get this over with, the quicker I can go back to bed and rest."

"Rest?"

She sighed. I'm about three months pregnant."

William made a face.

Mary rolled her eyes. "What did you expect? You're a negro man. You're not getting a popular non pregnant whore. I usually clean the girls bedding and what not. No man wants a pregnant whore, so I usually get dealt to men in debt or colored folks such as yourself. I am damaged goods."

William shook his head. "I find that impossible ma'am. You are beautiful."

Mary laughed. "You're mighty kind, William, but if you would...I want to get this over with." She reached for his pant's hem before William pushed her hand away.

"Wait. You still never told me about the black eye. Did someone hurt you?"

Mary bit her lip. "It was just the baby's father. I asked him to take care of the baby once it was born, and he beat me."

"No man should lay hands on a woman."

"Huh, you're daddy teach you that?"

William nodded. "He also told me to treat my woman like queens. If you were mine, I would treat you like one."

Mary laughed. "I'd like to see you try."

"If you give me the opportunity. I would turn your life around."

Mary chuckled. "How? You're a negro man in America. Your opportunity is limited because of the color of yours skin."

"Nah, where I come from you take what is yours. I earned the rank of Captain by taking. I killed every white man I could and lead negro men fearlessly into battle. I'm one of the best shooters too. Hell, even the angel of death is scared of me. Last I checked this was the Wild West. I can have anything I want. If I want it, I'd take it."

Mary smiled. "So, if you wanted me, you'd take me too?"

"Just say the word. I'd take you from this house, I'll rob a bank for you to have money for your baby, hell I'd even kill that asshole who hit you."

"So, if I asked you to do all those things, what would you want in return?"

William scratched his chin and replied. "Be my wife."

Mary laughed. "A white woman and black man as man and wife? You must have had too much whiskey."

"I'm serious. I would do all of those things for you if you make me your husband. Plus, as your husband, I would raise your baby like my own. Do we have a deal?"

Mary bit her lip. The idea was crazy. A white woman and black man married. No one had seen a thing. However, she was tired of having every stranger's prick inside her. She wanted her own bed, a house, maybe even a garden for crops. She didn't know the man but judging by his stronger character and broad muscular build she knew that he was a man of action. She couldn't explain it, but she trusted him.

A smile spread on her face as she nodded. "What the hell. You get killed trying to do all of that, I'd just end up back here. You do all of those things for me, you got a deal. So, what now?"

"Well, I usually agree to a partnership with a handshake or a contract, but given that you'd be my wife, I figured..."

"We seal our deal with sex?"

"I would be obliged." William grinned. He tossed his hat on a nearby table and then laid on the bed.

Mary smiled, and followed, straddling his waist. She shimmied his trousers down to his ankles, and then grasped his black cock. She stroked him softly until his dick ballooned in size. William groaned as a tingling sensation crawled up his toes to the rest of his body. Mary began jerking William with vigor. He groaned, arching his back from the pleasure.

She hiked her dress up and sat on top his hard cock. She moaned as she sunk down on his dark thick rod. Rocking her hips, she rode him like a horse. Below, William grinned watching Mary's pleasure grow. He held her hips, enjoying the show she gave him. He'd never had sex with a white woman before, but he was loving it so far. The complexion of his black fingers wrapped around pale thighs was a thing of beauty. Her skin was softer than the finest fur. Her skin was whiter than milk. Looking in her green eyes, William was a man possessed.

"Damn, woman..." He groaned.

"Does that feel good?"

"Yeah, it feels real good." He reached up to her dress and massaged her tits.

"You want me to lower my dress?"

He nodded. Mary smiled at him and then untied her dress. Lowering her outfit, she revealed her pale plump breasts upon him. William stared at her chest with wonder and his fingers brushed across her rouge-colored areolas. Her body shuddered from his touch.

"You got pink nipples." He uttered.

Mary laughed. "I do. Have you ever been with a white woman before?"

"You're my first. I'd tell you...this is some of the best sex of my life." He groaned tilting his head back. Her pussy felt tight and warm. Almost like a glove on a cold winter's day. She was wet too, the smooth slick friction of his dick sliding in and out her with ease was intoxicating. It made William roll his eyes back and speak in words and phrases he didn't recognize.

She giggled. "I'm enjoying myself too."

William grinned and grabbed her ass and increased his speed. Holding her, he pounded into her pussy, watching with awe as her breasts jiggled from the impact. Despite her enlarged stomach and black eye, William found Mary beautiful. Everything about her was pretty. Her red hair, the freckles covering her face and body, the way his dark fingers blended into her pale skin. It was like a perfect sunset.

Mary arched her back and moaned loudly.

"Oh, that's it William. Harder. Harder!" She commanded. "Uhhhh," she gasped. Her body tensed as she gasped for air. Watching her scream from her pleasure rose the hairs on his arms.

William could tell how much she enjoyed his time, she felt wetter than a puddle. She was better than any alcohol or drug he'd taken. That feeling he felt with her was one of a kind. He felt his own pleasure build. His cock throbbed from being inside her. Like a cork in a bottle, he was ready to pop. He didn't last long, as he came a few seconds later. He groaned as he emptied his seed inside her.

When he was done, he gasped for air and watched as Mary hopped off him. She too was sweaty and exhausted.

"Did you enjoy it?" She asked, tying her dress back up.

"That was some of the best sex I ever had." William hopped off the bed, cleaned his cock off from Mary's and his natural juices and then pulled his trousers up.

"Good. So did I," she grinned. "So, we have an agreement then? I will become your wife if you murder my baby's daddy and rob a bank?"

"Yes. Lure that son of bitch here tonight and I'd kill him. Be ready to leave right after. We'd be riding like hell afterwards."

"Why is that?"

"A black man killing a white man and riding away with his white baby's momma will put a price on my head quicker than than I can snap. I'd be a wanted man for a hangin."

"Okay, so I need to start packing now?"

"Yep, a small bag will do. After I shoot the fella, others will try and shot me. So be sure to protect yourself and the baby when the bullets start flying."

"Ain't going to happen. Remember they take guns before coming in, I'd steal some, plus everyone will be unarmed. Should help with our escape."

"Good point. So, it's just the guard that I'd worry about."

"Oh, Terry. Could you try not killing him. He's a good man."

William sighed. "Fine. I won't kill him. I'd knock him out, however anyone else who stops me will get a bullet in the head."

"Fine with me. As far as I'm concerned, it's their due."

"Alright. I'll see you tonight." William began to leave before Mary grabbed his hands.

"Wait," she said. William turned and was greeted by a passionate kiss from Mary. He was stunned as he felt the spark between them grow. When they broke apart, William breathed deeply, and Mary stroked his chin. "This is the sweetest thing any man as ever done for me. If you live up to your promise, I'd live up to mine. I'd be a good wife for you."

"Thank you, ma'am."

"Call me Mary."

William smiled and gave her a slight head nod before leaving her room.

Chapter 3

William watched the sun go down over the Pacific Ocean. It was beautiful, and he finally reached his dream of seeing the ocean. However, he had a new goal. He had a chance to start a new life, with a wife and potentially be a father to her child. He knew what he was about to do was suicidal. It was a steep price to pay for a wife, but he was willing to bet his life for it. He checked his guns and his ammo belt. Satisfied he grabbed the reins of his horse and rode towards the whore house.

Unlike last time, William didn't go to the back entrance. He walked towards the front of the building and was met with suspicious looks. However, William didn't care. He strolled up the steps of the deck and walked towards the front entrance. The guard at the front glared at William and spat tobacco at his feet.

"You must be lost boy. This establishment doesn't take niggers."

"That's funny, because I was just here a few hours ago."

"Bullshit. We don't let your kind in here."

"Really? Then should I talk to Madam Green, owner of this establishment? Or did you want me to walk around back to met you? I mean that is where the rest of your black clientele goes."

The guard eyes rose and his cheeks turned pink as he leaned forward and whispered, "listen here, boy, you about to make this a whole lot worse. If you keep jabbing about the back entrance, your kind ain't going to be welcome no..." Before he could say another word, William pulled out his gun and placed it in the man's chest.

"I'd finish those words carefully."

The others on the deck began to draw their own weapons but William shook his head and removed another gun from his holster. "Easy fellas. You shoot me, the first person who drops is Terry. You don't want that do you?"

"Listen boy, you only making it worse. Just leave and we won't do nothing," Terry growled.

"Ha, I know the minute I leave and your friends are going find me and string me up. I ain't no fool. No, I'm not taking any chances."

"So, what are you going to do?" Terry asked.

"We're going to walk in and get ourselves a drink. Come on." William walked forward with his gun still pointed at Terry's gut. Walking into the saloon, the noise quieted down when William and Terry walked in. Looking around, William spotted Mary serving drinks. She smiled when they made eye contact. William winked at her and then looked at the crowd.

"Evening ladies and gentlemen. I am looking for a Mister Alex Jenkins. Is Alex here?"

"Who wants to know?" A man stood up and asked. William looked towards Mary, who nodded, giving him the signal that this was the man he was supposed to kill. He smiled and blew her a kiss before turning to face the man who stood up.

"Well, I came to kill him. He's recently struck a woman that I'm in love with and I don't take kindly to it."

"You're a nigger how can you love…" before the man finished the sentence, William pulled the trigger and shot him in the head. Quickly he pistol whipped the Terry in the head, and shot another man next to him who was reaching towards his weapon.

He looked towards Mary and shouted, "run!" Mary took off running towards the door. Other men all stood up to attack William, but he was faster. He shot eight of them, before he was empty. He ducked behind the bar and began reloading. Mary was there, with three guns and a rifle.

"I'd figured you would need these."

"Well, I be... Can you shoot? There's about ten men between us and my horse."

Mary grinned, stood up from cover and shot two men before retreating back to cover.

William laughed. "I'm happy to see that my future wife is a good shot."

"I'm good at more than fucking." She joked.

"I can see. We're going to have to shoot our way out. On three we stand and run to my horse. It's tied on the right, it's brown and white. You can't miss her. Got it?"

Mary nodded.

"One, two, three," both stood up and unleashed a barrage of bullets. This gave the couple time to run out the saloon door to the waiting horse. William hopped on and helped Mary up. The crew of men fired behind them, but William and Mary were out of range as the horse ran like the wind.

Out of the town, Mary laughed as she tilted her head back. "What a rush!" she yelled.

"You're first gun fight?" William asked.

"Yes. Wow, now I see why men are always getting into them."

William laughed. "I'd seen enough to last me a lifetime in the war."

"A solider and an American hero." Mary leaned forward and placed her head on his back hugging him.

"I'm an outlaw now too. My name will me posted in every town, village and community. It's okay, though. I got what I wanted."

"Thank you for killing that man. Watching a bullet go through his brain felt like a weight was lifted off my shoulders."

"I told you. I do anything for my woman."

"Well, I told you I'd do anything to make sure my husband is happy."

"We ain't married yet. I still gotta rob a bank for you, Mary."

"Ahh, you're close enough for me." She reached down and grabbed his cock. "What do you say we settle in for the night?"

William chuckled. "I'd like that."

The couple found a small cave and made a fire. William rolled the sleeping blanket on the ground and Mary laid on top of it patting the area next to her. William sat near her, and she kissed him. The two made out as their clothes were taken off. William gasped, ogling nakedness, he still couldn't get over her beauty. He loved her redhair, the freckles on her pale body, her plump tits and her curvy waist. Everything to him was mesmerizing. Leaning forward, he kissed her once more. He rubbed her cheek and stared deep into her eyes.

"Lay down," he commanded.

Mary leaned back staring at him. William winked at her and disappeared between her legs.

"William what are you..." before she could ask, she felt his tongue on her outsides. She shrieked from the feeling as no one had ever licked her there. The way his tongue lapped at her insides was amazing. Her back arched as a tingling feeling shot through her toes to her core. She moaned loudly as her hand grabbed William's afro. Her hips buckled but William held her down, not stopping the powerful force that was taking over her. Mary leaned her head back and grabbed the blanket as the feeling grew. Like a wave it swept her off her feet as she moaned loudly.

"Uhhhh," she exclaimed. "Oh wow, we that was…"

William looked up and wiped his face. Mary rubbed his cheek and smiled. "That was amazing. I'd never came like that before. Where did you learn that?"

"Picked up that trick when I was stationed in New York."

"Damn. What you did with your mouth…no man had ever done that for me."

"Really, well now that your mine, I will always do it for you. You taste sweeter than honey." Mary grinned and kissed him. She smiled and rubbed his cheek once more.

"I want you in me."

"I want fuck you too. Turn around."

Mary grinned and shifted her position, with her ass facing him. He stroked his hardness and entered her from behind. He felt his hard cock enter her wet, tight pussy and he groaned from the erotic feeling. Grabbing her hips, he thrusted into her. She moaned from his passionate movements. Next to the fire, their bodies came together with a satisfying clap. They weren't fucking but they were making love as their bodies moved as one.

"Oh, William," she groaned. "You feel so good."

"You feel good too." William moaned. His hands massaged her ass. He noted how soft her skin felt in his hands. Every inch of her was beautiful and she was all his.

Mary couldn't believe what was happening. A few days ago, she was potentially going to be a single mother, but God found a way to change her fortunes. She made a choice to wed William and she hadn't regretted it yet. When she first met him, she knew he was strong and could deliver his promises. He saved her from that hell hole. She owed him. He'd held up his end of the bargain and she would happily hold up hers. There was something about William she couldn't put her finger on.

She could tell that he found her attractive. She did too. His dark skin, broad muscles and big black cock made her weak at the knees. Not to mention the sex. The way William made love was different. He wasn't overly aggressive or only cared about himself coming. The way he touched her, kissed her and massaged her, told a different story. Plus, there was that thing he did with his mouth. The way he moved his tongue on her insides was like an artist with a paint brush. He gave her pleasure, something that she'd rarely felt before.

"I'm nearly there." He grunted.

"Me too."

"You too?"

"You're cock. It's so big. Biggest I've ever had." She moaned. "It feels good inside me. Makes me enjoy the sex with you. You feel…Oh…" she shuddered as her body shook. William felt a warm liquid swell around his cock and he too finished. He groaned as he emptied his seed into her once more. When he was finished, he laid exhausted. Mary laid next to him, her head on his chest.

"That was amazing." She whispered.

"You truly enjoyed it?" He asked.

"I did. I've had sex with hundreds of men, you are the first that makes my body feel like that."

"What does it feel like?" He asked.

"It's hard to explain. It's a warm happy tingling feeling. It doesn't come often, but when it does." Mary breathed deeply. "It's amazing."

William smiled. "I'm glad you felt it."

"Thanks," Mary smiled and kissed William. "So, what's the plan. You murdered the man I wanted dead, now you must secure our future with money. How do you plan on doing that?"

"There's a gold mine not to far from here. A courier takes that gold and delivers it to the city. I ambush the route and we steal the gold."

"How much gold we talkin?"

"About $10,000."

Mary's eyes got wide hearing the large sum of money. "That would set us for life."

William nodded. "Plus, we'd can take those gold bars anywhere. Mexico would be the safest bet. We get to the border, and no U.S Marshalls going to set foot in that county."

"What about bounty hunters?"

"If they are foolish enough to come for me and what's mine, they will meet the end of my barrel. You're my mine now, that baby is mine now, and I will die protecting you both. I promise after this, we'd be free."

"Sounds good to me."

"Good. Get some rest because tomorrow we ride for our fortunes."

Chapter 4

The trap was set as William looked at Mary who was across the ridge waiting. She was his sniper with the rifle and had their horse. He blew a kiss at her and then took a deep breath as their crazy plan unfolded. Across the horizon he could see the stagecoach along with three other riders. William grabbed the fuse, and when the group got into range he lit the dynamite.

The ground shook from the huge explosion and the rocks from the mountains came tumbling down. William watched as the rockslide killed the riders and damaged the carriage. Once the coast was clear William whistled and Mary came down from the ridge with the horse.

"That was easier than I'd expected it to be. You done this before?" She asked.

"Several times, but not to rob anyone. During the war, I was apart of a special unit in the army. Our jobs were to sabotage supplies for the confederates."

"Oh, that makes sense."

"Yes, we were a small group of men behind enemy lines so we didn't want to draw attention ourselves. So, what we did was make it look like accidents. A fire here, a misfire explosion there. Make it look like an accident, people tend to ask less questions."

"Hence the rockslide."

William nodded. "We steal the gold and no will know what happened. They'd just assume that someone took it after their men were killed by a freak act of nature. Now help me load up the cart. We don't got long before someone comes along and spots the wreck.

After the couple gathered the gold, they got on their horse and rode into the sunset.

They'd been riding for a day before Mary asked William to stop.

"Is everything okay?" He asked.

"Everything is perfect."

"Good. We just have another day's ride, and we'd be in Mexico."

"I know but before we go, I want to tell you, I do."

"You do what?" He asked.

"I do accept your marriage. I am your wife, and you are my husband."

William grinned and kissed Mary. "Then I guess we should stop for the night and make this marriage official."

"I wouldn't have it any other way."

After setting up camp, Mary was getting the blanket ready for the night when William approached her.

"Mary?"

"Yes, husband?" She mocked.

William grinned. "Now, I don't have any rings, but I did make these from some yarn. I promise you when we get to Mexico, I'm going to get you a proper ring. That being said…" He got on one knee and Mary gasped. William grinned, took her hand and then placed the ring on her finger. "Mary, will you make me the happiest man in the world?"

"Yes! Of course, I will. You make me happy too." She replied.

William grinned and stood up. He grabbed her chin and gave her a passionate kiss. As they kissed, they fell on top of the blanket. William hiked up her skirt and lowered himself, eating her out once more. Mary loved that feeling. She loved the way his fat tongue lapped inside her insides. She loved the way he held her down and made her into a pile of goo. This man was hers and she couldn't be happier. The pleasure took hold of once more as she gasped. Her toes curled as she moaned, and her body twisted and turned from the one of kind feeling.

"Oh William," she moaned. "Oh, Oh, oh, uhhhhh…" she was in shock as her body exploded. She felt like she radiated like a thousand suns as she came. When she was through, she felt exhausted and gasped for air. William chuckled and pushed back a strand of her red hair.

"Are you okay?" He asked.

"Yes, I'm not sure what came over me. That was… wow."

"I'm glad you liked it."

"I'd like it more if I felt my husband's cock inside me."

"Your wish is my commanded." He kissed her and then got on top of Mary.

"Am I putting to much weight on you?"

Mary shook her head. "This is okay."

William grinned and kissed her again. Mary hastily untied William's trousers and pulled them down. He took the tip of his penis and lightly played with her opening. He teased her with his head as he lubed up the top of his cock with her juices. She bit her lip, watching him. William smiled at her before entering inside her. He groaned as he inserted through her tight warm wet hole. Rocking his hips, he began to thrust, and he leaned his head down to kiss her passionately.

They made love underneath the moon, not as strangers but as husband and wife. Something felt different about having sex with her. William couldn't describe it, but it felt more pleasurable. His emotions were full, and he couldn't help but to smile at his wife.

The couple soon shifted and Mary was on top, with William on bottom. Despite their new position, the couple never broke their lover's glances. Mary grabbed Williams legs as she rode him. Her moans were a wolf howls to the full moon. She felt like she was in heaven as she rode his cock.

"Oh Mary," William cried.

"William," she responded.

Both were wrapped in the pleasure from one another. William sat up and clutched Mary close. She kissed him and he groaned as he unleashed his seed into her her again. He continued to thrust into her until he was limp. When he was done, the couple laid together, looking at the moon above them.

"I love you," William whispered.

"I love you too," Mary grinned. She kissed him, and the newlyweds felt asleep in each other's arms.

The next day the couple rode into Mexico to start their new lives. Like William, Mary kept her promise. She was a good wife to him. The couple settled near the coast, allowing William to look at the Pacific Ocean anytime he wants and with the money the couple started a cattle ranch. Seven kids later, William and Mary never doubted their marriage or their decisions to become outlaws, in the country they once called home. To them the decision was worth it. In the end it brought them closer together and for that they're happy.

The End

I Like It Black Series

I Like It Black 2020 Blurb

Enjoy seven popular interracial erotica short stories written by Hunter Briggs in 2020, all featuring sexy black men, all having one thing in common, BBC.

Each story features elements of naughty Asian housewives, sexy matures, and wild cuckolds. Read all seven of these stories for one low price!

Includes Popular Stories Like:

Our Submissive Third

When HR manager, Brandon Johnson, receives a race discrimination case, he immediately faces difficulties with accused racist coworker, Savannah Davis. Enraged after listening to her disrespect his Korean wife and his own African American heritage, he wants her to be fired from the company. However, upon learning that she's a valuable asset to the business, Brandon has no choice but to allow her racist comments about him and his wife to go unanswered. Upset, he and his wife blackmail Savannah to be their submissive third in their bedroom. Will their plan work, or will it backfire in their faces?

The Entire Taken by the Black Billionaire Series, including, The Asian Housewife, The Russian Housewife and The Coworker's Wife

Leroy Potter is a rich, playboy billionaire, who doesn't take no for an answer. He lives by the motto that nothing is priceless, and applies that thought to his extravagant lifestyle, including the women he sleeps with. Unlike most men, Leroy doesn't like seducing gorgeous models or famous actresses, instead he goes after something considered forbidden fruit, married housewives!

Taken on my Wedding Day

I hate him.

If he thinks he could get away with this on the day before our wedding, he has another thing coming.

Oh, I'll get my revenge, I'll be damn sure about that. He's not going to like it either. Just downstairs, I've spotted three sexy black men that I plan on seducing. On this day, I will no longer belong to him. I will belong to them.

I will allow them to do anything they can imagine to me. And in the end, my hair will be in shambles, my dress will be torn, and my makeup will be smeared. I will no longer be his prize, I will be his used goods. I will no longer be his trophy wife, I will be his shame. As I walk down the aisle a mess, I will grin ear to ear, knowing that I am the one thing he despises most in this world, a white woman tainted by a black man.

I want to be presented in this way to him because this is how he made me feel. When I learned of his deceit, he ripped my heart out and tore it in two. Now, I shall do the same. When I walk down that aisle, I want him to know, I wasn't his on this day, I was theirs.

Read these stories and more in this tantalizing erotica anthology!

https://www.amazon.com/dp/B089FZCWFN

I Like It Black: Volume 3

The next erotic installment of the I Like it Black series is here. Read 17 stories, all featuring sexy black men, promising to fulfill all of your dirty fantasies.

Each story includes elements of naughty mature housewives, curvy BBWs, and wild cuckolds. With WWBM, AWBM, and IWBM pairings! Every story is a page turner and will have you craving for more until you get to the end.

Includes Popular Stories Like:

The Indian Housewife

In his next impossible sexual conquest, Leroy finds himself eating dinner at a small family run Indian restaurant owned by Abhijit and his beautiful wife, Radhika. Little does he know that the owners are in arrears and must pay a half a million dollar debt or they will lose everything to the bank. Upon learning that the billionaire is eating in their restaurant, Abhijit makes him an offer for an equity partnership in the restaurant. To Abhijit's surprise, Leroy counteroffers requiring a 50/50 partnership, and an agreement to share his wife with him as well! Will Abhijit agree to Leroy's terms or will his pride get in the way of saving his family from financial ruin?

The BBW and the Football Stud

Xavier Wallace could have any girl he wanted. As the star football player at the university, women practically beg to sleep him. Feeling confident in the night, his friends challenge him to a bet that couldn't sleep with a shy redhead bbw student at a party, Hannah Mack. Will Xavier win the bet, or will the challenge provide more than he bargained for?
This interracial WWBM erotic romance short story is approximately 3,800 words long and ends with a HEA. For mature 18+ readers only.

Rent Check

Caroline is desperate. With rent coming due in a matter of days, she must find a job or her family will be homeless. Despite being forty-two years old, she applies to a local strip club. To her surprise, she finds that the owner wants her for a date and is willing to pay for her her company. Little does she know that by the end of the night she will fall for his charm.
Rent Check is an erotic interracial WWBM short story romance at 7,000 words. It is for mature readers over 18 only.

And much much more!

These stories contain exotic material and should be read by mature readers over 18.

About the Author

Hunter Briggs is an interracial romance erotica author. He loves writing out of the box stories, that at are different from the rest. If you like reading about tall, dark and handsome alphas and beautiful, thick thighed women, then Hunter Briggs is the author for you. If he's not writing hot, burn a hole in your panties erotica, Hunter Briggs is lazily watching TV because he has no other cool hobbies like other authors. Hunter Briggs is a loving husband and father and while he owns no dogs, he has always wished for a furry friend. He enjoys anything that can raise his blood pressure including, spicy buffalo wings, onion rings and ice-cold beer.

Follow me on Twitter: @Briggs_Romance

Follow me on Amazon (Open the page, and click the yellow "+ Follow" button underneath the Hunter Biggs logo)